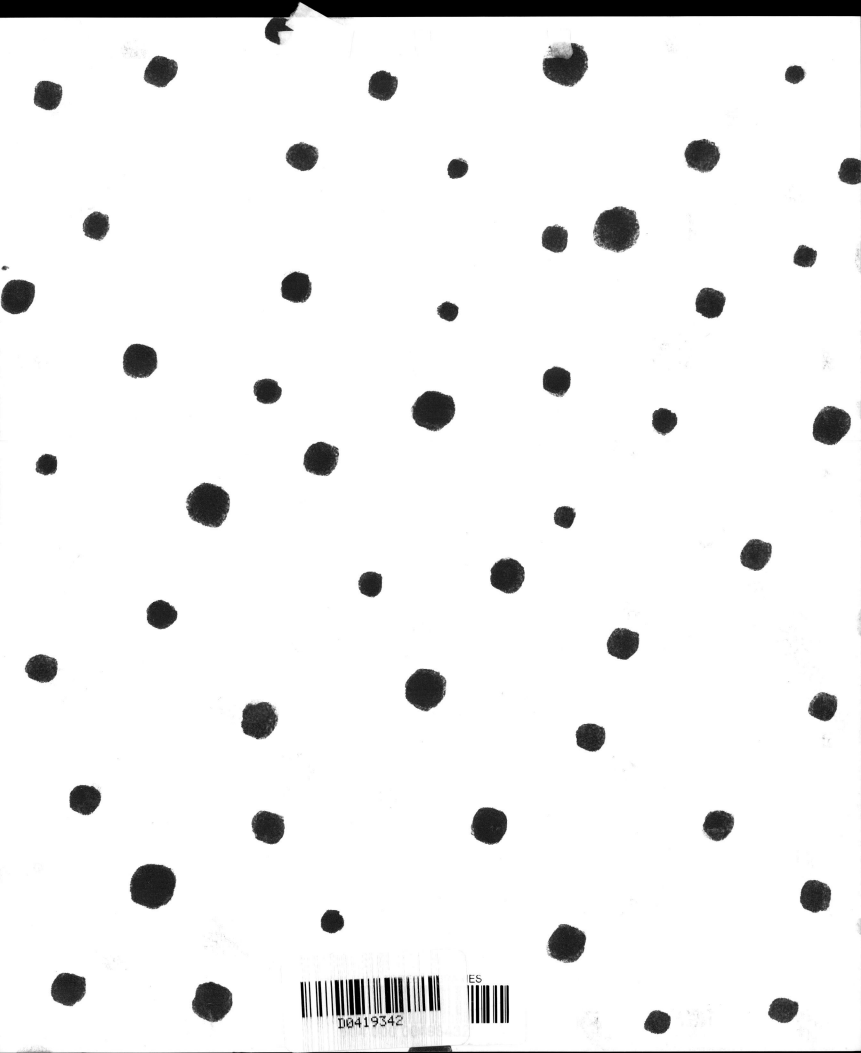

THE HUNDRED AND ONE Dalmatians

by
Dodie Smith

Adapted by **Peter Bently**

Illustrated by **Steven Lenton**

EGMONT

ONCE there were two Dalmatians named Pongo and Missis.

They lived with Mr and Mrs Dearly in a big house in London.

"Dear Pongo," said Missis one day. "We are going to have puppies!"

But Missis didn't have just **one** puppy.

Or two.

Or three.

She had **fifteen!**

The biggest puppy was Patch. He looked after tiny Cadpig, the smallest puppy of all.

Lucky was the bravest.

And Roly Poly made everyone laugh.

One afternoon, a woman came to the house.
Her name was Cruella de Vil.

"What delightful dogs!"
declared Cruella.
"I will buy them all."

"We'll never
sell them," said
Mr Dearly firmly.

"Pity," muttered Cruella as she left.
"They would make an enchanting fur coat."

Pongo growled.

"I don't like Cruella de Vil," he said.

"Nor do I," said Missis. "She's enough to frighten the spots off a pup!"

Not long afterwards, Pongo and Missis went out for a walk, but when they returned they had a nasty shock . . .

Where were the puppies?

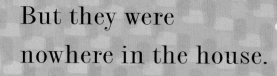

"Perhaps they're hiding," said Pongo.

But they were nowhere in the house.

"My poor pups have been **stolen!**" wailed Missis.

Mr and Mrs Dearly called the police.

They put adverts in the newspapers.

But it was no use. The puppies had vanished!

That evening, Pongo and Missis sat on
a nearby hill and barked.

"Help!" they cried.
"Fifteen Dalmatian
puppies stolen!"

Many dogs heard them.
But no one had
seen the puppies.

But then, from far away, they heard an old sheepdog.
"I have seen your puppies," he barked, gruffly.
"They are at a house called Hell Hall!"

"We must go there and rescue
them!" said Missis.

"You're right!" said Pongo. "We will leave tonight!"

When the Dearlys were asleep, Pongo and Missis
slipped silently from the house.

They ran through the freezing streets and out into the countryside.
On and on they went, through sleeping villages and frosty fields.

At last they reached Hell Hall. The old sheepdog
greeted them warmly. His name was the Colonel.

"What a frightening house!" said Missis.

"It belongs to a woman named Cruella de Vil," said the Colonel.

"I knew it!" said Pongo. "Cruella stole our puppies!"

The house was surrounded by a high wall.
How would the dogs get in?

The Colonel knew a way. He led Pongo
and Missis into an old tower.

When they reached the top,
Missis peeped out and gasped.

She could see her puppies –
and dozens more!

"Cruella has been collecting
Dalmatian puppies," said the Colonel.
"She wants to make them all
into spotty fur coats."

"Then we must save them all!" said Missis.

Two men came out of the house.
"That's Saul and Jasper," said the Colonel.
"They are guarding the pups for Cruella.
But they spend most of their time
watching television."

That evening, Pongo and Missis crept up to the house.
"There's **Lucky!**" cried Missis.

"**Mum!** Dad!" exclaimed Lucky.
"We knew you'd rescue us!

Come on, I'll take
you to the others.
If we're quiet, Saul and Jasper
won't notice a thing."

Suddenly they heard a voice outside the door.

"Saul! Jasper! Where are you?"

Pongo and Missis froze. They had heard that voice before . . .

It was Cruella de Vil!

"The whole country is looking for those pups!" snarled Cruella. "I want you to make them into spotty fur coats tonight!" She slammed the door and went upstairs to bed.

"It'll take ages to round up all these pups!" grumbled Jasper. "Let's watch some more TV first."

"Now's our chance to escape," whispered Pongo, as he and Missis silently led the pups out through a kitchen window.

On the way, they ate everything in sight. "Cruella won't have any breakfast!" laughed Pongo.

"Serves her right," said Missis.

Soon the Dalmatians were all
out of the tower and on the
other side of the wall.

"Cruella is sure to come after you," said the Colonel.
"You must leave at once."

"It's a long way home," frowned Missis. "The puppies are too small to walk all that way. Especially Cadpig."

"Don't worry," smiled the old sheepdog. "Cadpig can ride in this toy cart!"

"Good idea," said Pongo.

"Thanks for your help!" said Missis.

"My pleasure," said the Colonel. "Goodbye – and good luck!"

The Dalmatians raced
bravely through the night.
But it wasn't long before the
puppies grew cold and exhausted.
And then it started to snow.

"We'll never make it to London,"
sighed Pongo.

TOOT! TOOT!

"That's Cruella's car!" cried Missis.
"It's coming this way!"

Cruella was getting closer. But there was nowhere to hide.

Then Missis spotted a big van parked nearby. And sitting in the back of the van was a little terrier.

"Help!" barked Pongo.
"We're being chased!"

"You're the missing Dalmatians!" said the terrier. "Quick, jump in!"
The Dalmatians scrambled into the van just in time.

DE V1L

Cruella zoomed
right past them . . .

"Look!" cried Missis. "She's skidding!"

CRASH!

Cruella's car slid off the
road into a ditch.

DEVIL

"Right," chuckled the terrier. "My driver's heading to London. Need a lift?"

"Yes please!" said Pongo and Missis.

It was snowing heavily outside when
Mr and Mrs Dearly heard barking.

They dashed to the door –
and in ran dozens of Dalmatians!

"It's Pongo and Missis and their puppies!" cried Mr Dearly.

"And many more puppies besides!" said Mrs Dearly.

And they started to count them all.

101

As the Dearlys finished counting, the clock struck midnight.

"It's Christmas Day," said Mrs Dearly.

"Well done, Pongo and Missis!"

"We've got the best
Christmas present ever."

One hundred and one Dalmatians!

For Tara, who loves dogs.
P.B.

For the stupendous Steven Butler x
S.L.

EGMONT
We bring stories to life

The Hundred and One Dalmatians first published in Great Britain in 1956
by William Heinemann Ltd. Original picture book adaptation edition first published
in 2017 under the title *The Hundred and One Dalmatians* by Egmont UK Limited.
The Yellow Building, 1 Nicholas Road, London, W11 4AN.
Original text copyright © Pongo and Missis Ltd 1956
Text adaptation copyright © Pongo and Missis Ltd 2017
Text adapted by Peter Bently from the original title *The Hundred and One Dalmatians*
written by Dodie Smith.
Illustrations copyright © Steven Lenton 2017
The illustrator has asserted his moral rights.
All rights reserved.

ISBN 978 1 4052 8165 2 (hardback)
ISBN 978 1 4052 8166 9 (paperback)

A CIP catalogue record for this title is available from the British Library